# JAMES STEVENSON

# The
# Worst Person's
# Christmas

Greenwillow Books, New York

Printed in Hong Kong by
South China Printing
Company (1988) Ltd.
First Edition
10 9 8 7 6 5 4 3 2 1

Library of Congress
Cataloging-in-Publication Data

Stevenson, James (date)
     The worst person's Christmas / by James Stevenson.
          p.       cm.
     Summary: The worst person particularly dislikes
Christmas until his neighbors' kindness
triggers a happy accident that forces him
to participate in the holiday festivities.
     ISBN 0-688-10210-7 (trade)
     ISBN 0-688-10211-5 (lib.)
     [1. Christmas—Fiction.]    I. Title.
PZ7.S84748Wne       1991
[E]—dc20
90-39716       CIP       AC

The worst person in the world didn't like anything anybody else liked. He didn't like springtime, or music, or dessert, or laughing, or people who were friendly.

He didn't like his dog, Daisy, and Daisy didn't like him.
Whenever the worst walked by, Daisy growled.

Sometimes she nipped his pants and wouldn't let go.

"I'm thinking of trading you in for a cat," the worst would say.

But what the worst person hated most of all was Christmas.

A few days before Christmas there was a big snowstorm.
The worst looked out at the falling snow.
"This should cause a lot of problems for Christmas
shoppers," he said to Daisy.

In the morning the snow had stopped.

The worst person came out
carrying an old tennis racket.

He whacked the snow
off all his signs.

"That's better," he said.

The worst looked at his mailbox.

"I hope I didn't get any Christmas cards," he said.

He opened his mailbox. There weren't any. "Good," he said.

"Would you like me to shovel a path up to your house,
  Mr. Worst?" said Gordon, who lived down the block.
"How much?" said the worst.
"Ten cents," said Gordon.
"Robber!" said the worst. "I'll do it myself."

He went down to his cellar to get his old snow shovel.

At last he found it. "Good as new," he said.

As soon as he began to shovel,
the handle snapped.

"I'm going to take this right back
to the hardware store," he said.

He passed the Moffets' house, where the family
was stringing blue lights on a tree.
"Kind of cheerful, don't you think?" called Mr. Moffet.
"Waste of electricity," said the worst.

In the village loudspeakers were playing "Silent Night."
Mrs. Wilson said, "Christmas carols make
me all shivery and warm."
"Perhaps you should see a doctor," said the worst.

He almost bumped into Santa Claus.
"Watch it, Fatso," said the worst.

At the hardware store the worst said, "You sold me
a bad shovel. I want my money back."
The man said, "We haven't sold that kind of shovel
for forty years. Sorry, Mr. Worst."
"Rip-off!" said the worst.

The worst threw away
the shovel and
headed home.

"A bunch of us are going around singing
Christmas carols tonight," said Mr. Feltzer.
"How about joining us, Mr. Worst?"
"If I want to sing sappy songs, I don't have to
stand out in the slush to do it," said the worst.
"Just a thought," said Mr. Feltzer.

"We're having the neighbors over tomorrow afternoon,"
said Mrs. Wilson. "Cookies and punch.
Hope you'll come!"
"Extremely unlikely," said the worst.

He ran into Walker and Jenny, who lived next door.

"Look what Walker made in school, Mr. Worst," said Jenny.

"What is it?" said the worst.

"A birdhouse," said Walker. "For my mommy and daddy's Christmas."

"Well," said the worst, "it's not too late to buy something at the store."

Walker and Jenny watched the worst march into
his house and slam the door.
"At Christmas," said Walker, "he's more awful
than usual."
"Maybe it's because he doesn't get any presents,"
said Jenny.

"We could give him a present," said Walker.

"What would he like?" said Jenny.

"He wouldn't like anything," said Walker.

"That's the problem."

"How about a fruitcake?" said Jenny.

"He *is* a fruitcake," said Walker.

"Perfect," said Jenny.

That night the worst put a chair by his front window so that, when the carol singers came, he could tell them to get off his property and go away.

He waited for an hour. "Where *are* those nincompoops?" he said to himself.

Half an hour later he heard singing in the distance.

"Here they come at last," he said. He got ready to yell.

The carolers approached.

"Let's skip the worst's house," said Mr. Feltzer.

"He doesn't like Christmas carols."

"It would just annoy him," said Mrs. Moffet.

They all walked quietly past his house.

"I guess they know better than to try to sing in front
of *my* house," said the worst. "Lucky for them!"

He went to bed, but he couldn't sleep. A soft blue light was coming through the window.

It was the tree in front of the Moffets' house.

He got dressed, went over, and knocked on the Moffets' door.

"Why, it's Mr. Worst!" said Mrs. Moffet. "Merry Christmas!"

"Never mind the soft soap," said the worst.

"Your tree is keeping me awake."

He went back to bed, but he still couldn't sleep.

It was very dark now and very quiet.

The next afternoon Walker and Jenny brought a fruitcake
to the worst's house.

Jenny knocked on the door.
"I'm not home!" yelled the worst. "I went to Florida!"
"Let's get out of here," whispered Walker.

They left the fruitcake on his doorstep and ran to hide.

The worst opened the door and saw the fruitcake.

"Ha!" he said. "I'll just run that right down to the garbage can."

He put on his hat and coat and picked up the fruitcake.

He was stepping off his porch, when...

he slipped on the steps.
"Oh-oh," said Jenny.

The worst flopped
onto Walker and Jenny's sled . . .

and went careening down the hill, past his signs
and mailbox and garbage can, and along the street.

"Where do you think he's going?" said Walker.
"I don't know," said Jenny, "but he's going
    there awfully fast. Come on."

The party at the Wilsons' was underway when
suddenly there was a thud. The door flew open,
and in came the worst.

"Look who's here!" said Mrs. Wilson.

"I didn't mean to..." the worst began.
"Better late than never!" said Mrs. Wilson.

"And he's brought a lovely present, too!" said Mrs. Wilson.
"Have some cookies, Mr. Worst," said Mrs. Feltzer.
"Have some punch," said Mr. Moffet.

An hour later the worst went home, pulling Walker and Jenny's sled. He was humming something that sounded a little bit like "Jingle Bells."

Daisy nipped his pants. "I suppose you think you'll get a dog biscuit," said the worst.

"Now, don't expect one every single day,"
he said. "Christmas is special."